To SASHA

A Mystery Message

by Alexa Pearl

illustrated by Paco Sordo

little bee books

Contents

Up in the Air

"Follow me!" Wyatt called out to Sasha.

Wyatt galloped across the field. It had rained for days in Verdant Valley, but the sun had finally come out this afternoon. Raindrops still sparkled on the emerald-green grass.

"Do everything I do," said Wyatt.

"I will do it better!" Sasha galloped behind him.

Wyatt made a sharp turn. Sasha made a sharp turn.

He ran in a zigzag. Sasha ran in a zigzag.

Wyatt jumped over a log. Sasha jumped over a log.

Her best friend ran fast. Sasha ran fast, too.

Then she looked up. Oh, no! They were racing toward a big rock.

Is he going to jump over it? she wondered. The rock was so tall!

Wyatt ran directly at it. Faster and faster.

Sasha opened her mouth to cry out when—

Wyatt leaped!
Sasha held her breath.
Wyatt made it over.

Sasha exhaled—but then the rock was in front of *her*. She wasn't ready to jump. Instead, she was about to crash into it!

She had only one choice. Her wings opened wide, and she rose up into the air. She soared above the rock. A moment later, her hooves hit the ground behind it.

Wyatt whirled around. "No fair! You cheated."

"Me? No way," said Sasha. "I don't cheat."

"Flying is cheating," said Wyatt.

"Since when?" asked Sasha.

"Since you can fly and I can't," he said. "You have to stay on the ground for this game. Otherwise, it's totally unfair."

Sasha was a flying horse. She had beautiful wings with sparkly feathers.

Sometimes Sasha still couldn't believe she could fly. Nothing was more fun than flying. But her best friend Wyatt didn't have wings.

"Cross my wings, I'll play fair," Sasha promised. "Even without flying, I can do anything you can."

"We'll see about that!" Wyatt ducked under a low tree branch. Sasha ducked under the branch, too. He took four steps backward.

"Tricky!" cried Sasha. She walked backward, too.

Wyatt galloped across the meadow. The white patch on the center of Sasha's back began to itch. She kept galloping. The itching grew stronger. She knew what the itching meant. It meant her body wanted to fly!

No, thought Sasha. She'd promised Wyatt she wouldn't fly.

She closed her eyes, trying to make the feeling pass. *No flying, no flying,* she chanted to herself.

Slowly . . . slowly . . . the itchiness faded.

"Sasha! You're cheating again!"

Sasha's eyes snapped open at the sound of Wyatt's voice. She twisted her head to the right and to the left, searching for her friend.

"Down here!" Wyatt called from the ground below.

Sasha was up in the sky—and she was flying! She hadn't flapped her wings or taken off. What was happening?

The Golden Envelope

Sasha spotted two silver horses in the sky with her. Their metallic coats glinted in the sun. Sasha felt a powerful force coming from the two horses. Somehow, these horses had magically lifted her off the ground and brought her up to them!

♦ 13 ♦

"Who are you?" she called.

"We're the Royal Guards," said one horse. "We've been sent by the King and Queen."

"We've come for the Lost Princess of the Flying Horses," said the other horse.

"That's me." Sasha was part of a family of royal horses. "Why did you pull me up here? You made me lose the game."

Princess Sasha

"We can't land in Verdant Valley."
The first horse nodded toward the field
where Wyatt stood. "We must stay in
the clouds to guard the sky."

"We've come to give you this." The
second horse waved his thick tail, and
a large golden envelope appeared. It
floated between them. In the center of
the envelope was written: *Princess Sasha.*

"What's this?" asked Sasha.

"A very important invitation," said the first horse. "Super-special. Just for you."

Sasha's pale eyes lit up. Invitations meant parties—and Sasha *loved* parties.

She reached for the envelope. It glided to the right—she tried again. It hovered just beyond her reach.

The envelope is playing a game, thought Sasha. *Well, I can be tricky, too.*

She reached out her left front hoof and then—*surprise!*—clamped down quickly with her right front hoof, pinning the envelope between them.

"Got it!" Sasha couldn't wait to see what was inside of it. She put it between her teeth to rip it open.

Sasha tugged and tugged. The paper wouldn't tear!

"You can't rip open the invitation," said one of the silver horses.

"How do I open it?" asked Sasha.

"One petal at a time," said the other silver horse.

"What petals?" Sasha didn't see flowers anywhere.

The silver horses didn't answer her question. Instead, one said, "But do hurry. The invitation will disappear if you don't open it by sunset."

Then they flew away through the thin clouds.

Sasha stared at the mysterious golden envelope in wonder. Now what?

Petal Power

Sasha held the envelope tightly between her teeth. She flew back down to Wyatt.

"It's an invitation from the King and Queen," said Sasha. She placed the envelope between them on an old tree stump.

"Is it for a party?" asked Wyatt. "A show? A concert? A royal sporting event?"

"No idea," said Sasha. "It won't open. There's no flap to lift or anything. It's shut tight."

"Let me try." Wyatt took a deep breath. His cheeks puffed out. *Whoosh!* He let out a huge breath of air onto the envelope.

"Ewww! Did you just spit on it?" asked Sasha.

"I didn't spit. Well, not on purpose." He wiped off any slobber on the envelope with his tail. "I thought I could blow it open. You know, huff and puff and all that stuff."

"That only works for a house and a wolf." Sasha was silent for a moment, thinking. Then she called out, "Open, sesame!"

The envelope stayed shut.

"Open, cinnamon raisin!" said Wyatt. "Open, whole wheat!"

"What?" Sasha tilted her head.

"They're kinds of bagels, too. Isn't that what we're doing?"

"No. 'Open, sesame' is a magic phrase," she explained. "Do you know any other magic words that might open things?"

"I'm not the magic horse here," Wyatt reminded her. "That's your thing."

"True. But I don't know what to do." Sasha groaned.

Wyatt inspected the envelope again. "Did you see this?"

In the center of the envelope was a drawing of a flower.

"That's so weird." Sasha wrinkled her nose. "That flower wasn't here before."

"The flower has five petals," Wyatt pointed out. "Each one is a different color." One petal was fuchsia, one was sunburst orange, one was saffron yellow, one was lavender, and one was teal.

"The Royal Guard told me to open the envelope one petal at a time. These must be the petals!" Sasha pressed her hoof against them.

The envelope stayed shut.

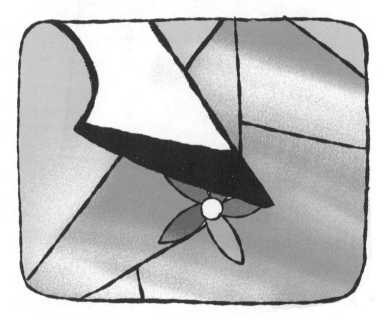

She touched each petal, one at a time. "They feel kind of sticky, but nothing's happening."

Wyatt gave the fuchsia petal a lick with his tongue. "Woweee, super-spicy!"

"Why did you taste it?" asked Sasha. Sometimes Wyatt did the craziest things.

"You lick an envelope to close it. I thought I could lick it to open it," said Wyatt. "But it didn't work."

Sasha and Wyatt tried blowing on the petals.

Then they tried rubbing the petals with their noses.

They tried swishing their tails across the petals.

The envelope still wouldn't open.

"I'm out of ideas. It's snack time." Wyatt strolled over to a patch of flowers and munched a daisy.

Sasha rolled her eyes. "Food is not more important than a royal invitation!"

"I'm *royally* hungry." Wyatt pulled off a heart-shaped petal from a big fuchsia flower and chewed. "Wow! This tastes just like the fuchsia petal on the envelope." Wyatt bit off another petal.

"Stop! Don't chew it!" Sasha's eyes grew wide. "That petal is the same color as one on the envelope."

"So what?" Wyatt wanted to keep eating.

"We should collect real petals, ones that match the five on the envelope." Sasha was excited by her plan. "I think real petals are the key to opening the invitation!"

"So, I can't eat this one anymore?" asked Wyatt.

"Sorry." Sasha nodded at a blue cornflower. "Here, eat this one. They taste the same."

Wyatt snorted. Blue flowers did *not* taste like fuchsia flowers. Fuchsia flowers were much sweeter and carried a hint of cinnamon. But Wyatt wanted to help his friend, so he dropped the fuchsia petal onto the ground. He gobbled up the blue flower in one bite.

"We need to find the other four petals," said Sasha. "It's time for a flower hunt!"

CHAPTER 4) Flower Hunt

"I know the perfect spot to look for flowers," said Wyatt.

"The field beyond the big trees," finished Sasha

"Exactly!" Wyatt raised his hoof for a hoof-bump.

Sasha trotted over to the cottonwood tree where her family lived. Her mother and father weren't there. They were down by the stream. And her two older sisters were off playing by the big rock.

Perfect! Sasha thought to herself. She was completely alone.

Sasha poked her nose high in the cottonwood tree. There was a nest where two baby birds had once hatched. One day, they flew away with their mother. Sasha waited and waited for them to come back, but they never did.

Sasha hid the invitation and the petal in the empty nest.

She strapped on her turquoise backpack and galloped quickly back to Wyatt. Together, they hurried through the big trees. The trees only let magical horses pass. Sasha was magical—and if Wyatt held tight to her tail, they let him through, too.

Best-friend privileges. That's what Sasha called it.

Rows and rows of flowers greeted them on the other side of the trees. Sasha saw flowers in amazing colors she couldn't even name. Rosy plum with a hint of sweet tangerine. Eclipse yellow ringed by periwinkle. Deep crimson combined with blizzard blue.

"We can find every petal we need right in this field!" cried Wyatt. "Easy breezy!"

"Let's hope so. We need a sunburst orange petal first," said Sasha.

"Over here." Wyatt nodded to a tall flower with petals folded into its middle.

Sasha gave one petal a soft tug.

"Eee-ow!" A high-pitched cry came from inside the flower. Then a tiny hand opened the petals. A small purple face peered out. It was a plant pixie!

"You woke me from my nap." The pixie rubbed the sleep from her eyes.

"I'm so sorry. I didn't know this flower was your home," said Sasha. Plant pixies lived inside flowers.

"I need my beauty rest." The plant pixie pulled the petals closed around her and disappeared back into the flower. "Be sure to knock next time."

Sasha turned to pull a petal from a flower growing nearby.

"Ouch!" A plant pixie popped its head out of this flower, too. She tilted her pointy face toward Sasha. "What's the big deal?"

Sasha felt horrible. She'd woken up *another* plant pixie. "Sorry. Are there plant pixies napping inside all these flowers?"

"Totally. It's siesta time." The plant pixie yawned and reached to close up her flower.

"Wait! All we need is one petal." Wyatt jumped in. "One petal and you can go back to sleep."

"No can do," said the plant pixie. "If you knock down the wall of a building, what happens? The whole building crumbles, that's what. These flowers are our homes. The petals are our walls."

"Please?" asked Wyatt. "Just one?"

"No, Wyatt," said Sasha. "These flowers belong to the plant pixies. We have to find flowers that grow in a field that isn't enchanted."

The plant pixie snuggled happily into her flower. "Many thanks, winged horse."

"Let's go back to Verdant Valley. It isn't magical there at all," said Sasha.

Wyatt thought about all the flowers he'd eaten. "I ate sunburst orange flowers on Mystic Mountain once. We'll need to climb to the top to get them."

Mystic Mountain's peak reached high into the clouds.

"I say we fly instead. Come on, Wyatt." Sasha's eyes twinkled. "Pretty please with a flower on top? And a carrot and an apple, too!"

Wyatt and Sasha soared up, up, up to the top of Mystic Mountain.

Wyatt stood on a huge, magic, flying leaf. The King and Queen had given it to him so he could fly with Sasha. It was the best present *ever*.

Wyatt touched down and hurried over to a patch of sunburst orange flowers. The petals were open wide. No plant pixies slept inside. It would be easy to pluck a petal here.

"Um, Wyatt." Sasha touched his back with her wing. "We're not alone."

Three baby mountain lions sat in the flower patch. They licked their tawny-brown fur with their little pink tongues. Their whiskers twitched. Their deep-blue eyes stared up at the two horses.

"Awwww! They're so cute. They're little balls of fluff." Wyatt started to nudge them out of the way.

"Don't do that." Sasha's eyes darted from side to side. "Mama mountain lion must be away getting food. If we touch her babies, she'll hurry back and pounce! Mountain lions are fierce."

Wyatt stepped away. "Is she close?"

"I don't know." The hairs on Sasha's mane prickled. There were many rocks and trees to hide behind. Mama mountain lion could be anywhere. Was she watching them right now?

"Hey there, kitties." Wyatt spoke in his sweetest voice. "Do me a favor, will you? Hand me one of those flowers. Please?"

They blinked up at him.

"Pluck the stem with your teeth. Come on, it's easy," said Wyatt. "You can do it."

The mountain lion cubs still didn't reach for any flower.

"Maybe they're not supposed to talk to strangers," said Sasha.

"How will we get a petal then?" asked Wyatt.

"I have an idea. I'll get the cubs away from the flower patch. You grab a petal super-fast, okay? Then we get out of here as quick as we can before mama mountain lion shows up."

Wyatt pawed the ground. "Okay. I'm ready."

With a *whoosh*, Sasha opened her wings. Her feathers glittered and sparkled in the sunlight. The cubs stared in amazement. They had never seen a horse with wings.

Sasha lifted off the ground. She flew above their heads. "Try to catch me."

Sasha flew away from the flower patch. The three cubs scampered after her. They swiped at her with their little paws, playing her game. Her plan was working.

"Now!" cried Sasha. Wyatt lunged toward the flowers.

At that moment, they heard a deep growl. Mama mountain lion was back!

CHAPTER 6) Bee Sting

Mama mountain lion raced toward Wyatt.

"Get on your leaf!" cried Sasha.

Wyatt's knees shook. He had to get away—fast. He searched for his flying leaf. Where had he left it?

"Hurry!" Sasha's heart thumped wildly. The mountain lion moved closer.

"Found it!" Wyatt pulled the leaf out from under a bush. He quickly unrolled it in front of him.

The mountain lion was closing in, but Wyatt hopped onto the leaf. As he rose into the air, Wyatt leaned over and plucked a sunburst orange petal with his teeth.

"You did it!" cried Sasha.

Mama mountain lion jumped at Wyatt. But she couldn't jump high enough. Wyatt flew safely above her head and waved to the surprised mama. Sasha waved to the cubs. Wyatt pushed the petal inside Sasha's backpack, then the two friends flew away from Mystic Mountain.

"Gosh, that was close. We have two petals. We need three more to open the invitation," said Wyatt.

"Saffron yellow is the next petal we need," said Sasha.

"What color is that?" asked Wyatt.

"It's a golden yellow-orange. Saffron is a spice," explained Sasha. "The sunflowers that grow by Kimani's cave are saffron yellow."

Kimani lived with the herd of flying horses in a magical land called Crystal Cove. To get to Crystal Cove, they had to walk through the big trees, across the field of enchanted flowers, take the ferry across a large lake, and hike down a beach covered in jewels and gems.

The journey took a long, long time without wings.

But Sasha didn't have time to wait. She wanted to open her invitation *now*. They would have to fly.

Soon, Sasha and Wyatt landed on the beach in Crystal Cove. The flying horses lived inside caves that lined the beach.

"Which one is Kimani's?" asked Wyatt.

"The one that's decorated in violet and has a bunch of fluffy pillows." Kimani's coat, mane, and braided tail were also violet.

Kimani let out a happy whinny when she spotted her friends. They told her all about the royal invitation.

"Here are the sunflowers." A patch of enormous saffron-yellow sunflowers grew by her cave door.

"These are A+ flowers," said Wyatt.

"Bees," said Sasha.

"Really? I could go with A-minus, but giving them a B seems harsh—"

"No, not that kind of B. Bumblebees," said Sasha.

A swarm of bees buzzed around the sunflowers.

"Yikes!" Wyatt backed away. "We'll get stung if we try to get the third petal from these."

"We can wait until it gets dark," suggested Sasha. "Bees go back to their hive at night."

"You can't wait," said Kimani. "Magic messages from the King and Queen disappear if they're not opened fast."

"Oh, I'd forgotten," said Sasha. "I have to get that third petal *now*."

She pushed her face toward the biggest sunflower—and a bee stung Sasha right on her nose.

CHAPTER 7) Catch that Bird!

"Owww!" Sasha hurried away from the sunflower. Her nose really hurt!

Kimani quickly mixed pineapple pulp with earthworm slime. She rubbed it on Sasha's nose. A minute later, the bee's sting stopped hurting.

"It's my magic recipe." Kimani showed her a small pot filled with gooey earthworms and sweet pulp. She tucked it into Sasha's backpack for later.

"Thank you, Kimani," Sasha said. She held up a saffron-yellow petal. "Look what I got." She'd plucked it just before the bee had got her. Wyatt put it in her backpack. "Now we need the lavender petal."

"This shouldn't be hard. The meadow is filled with lavender flowers." Kimani showed them the way.

"What happened?" cried Kimani when she saw the rows and rows of empty stems in the meadow. It seems a herd of zebras had eaten every lavender flower!

"Wait! There's one left," whispered Wyatt. He didn't want the hungry zebras to hear. They had missed one lavender flower in the corner of the meadow.

"Yippee!" Sasha cantered toward it. There were no plant pixies, no mountain lions, and no stinging bees in her way.

Just then, a huge bird spotted the lavender flower, too. He swooped down from the sky. He grabbed it with his beak and flew away.

"Seriously?" Sasha was annoyed. "That was *my* flower."

Sasha flew after the bird. He swooped and dipped. Sasha swooped and dipped, too.

Could she catch him before he ate her flower?

The bird glided on the wind. His big body soared.

Sasha flapped her wings as hard as she could. She thought about stopping. But if she did, she'd have to search for a new lavender petal. That would take time that she didn't have. The royal invitation might disappear.

She made herself fly faster. Soon, she was side by side with the bird.

"Excuse me? I need that flower," she called to him.

He shook his head.

"Please? I'll trade you something for it," she said.

He looked at her with interest.

Sasha's mind whirled. What could she trade? The only thing up here were clouds and rainbows. What did she have that a bird would want?

"My backpack!" cried Sasha. "There's a yummy, wriggling treat inside for you."

The bird poked his beak inside. He was surprised to find a pot filled with earthworms. They were yummier than a flower. He dropped the lavender flower in the backpack and took out a worm. What a great trade!

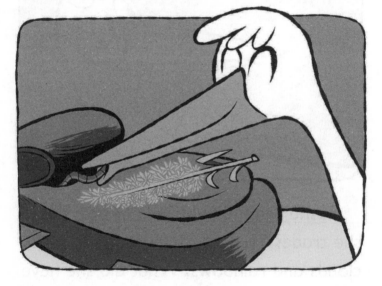

Sasha flew down to Wyatt and Kimani. "Got it! That leaves just one more petal to go."

The three friends went to look for a teal petal.

"What color is teal?" asked Wyatt.

"Blue-green," said Sasha.

"Green-blue," said Kimani.

"I've never seen a flower that color," said Wyatt.

On the beach, a spider monkey zipped by on a scooter. The horses asked if he'd seen a teal flower. He shook his head and scooted along.

They asked a flamingo spinning a Hula-Hoop. The flamingo shook her head and kept spinning.

They asked six rabbits nearby who were playing jump rope.

"Yes," said one white rabbit in the middle of the group.

"What? Really? Where?" cried Sasha.

8) Jump, Flutter

The jump rope slapped the ground as two rabbits continued to twirl it. The white rabbit stood in the center. He jumped and jumped.

"Please tell us where the teal flower is," begged Kimani.

The rabbit smirked at them. He hopped and hopped.

Time was running out. Sasha kicked out her hoof and stopped the twirling rope. "I need to know. There's this invitation and—"

"I'll tell you if you win," said the white rabbit.

"Win what?" asked Wyatt.

"A jump rope contest. Me against"— he looked at the group of horses—"any one of you. The most jumps wins."

"That's not fair," said Sasha. "How can a horse out-jump a rabbit?"

The white rabbit shrugged. "Then I guess no teal flower for you."

Kimani nudged Sasha. "Look, we have to try at least."

Sasha knew her friend was right. They were so close to getting all five petals. "Fine. I'll be the jumper."

Two rabbits held one long jump rope. Two other rabbits held another long jump rope. The white rabbit and Sasha each stood in the middle of a rope.

"Ready?" asked the white rabbit.

"Ready." Sasha sounded more confident than she felt. Jumping up and down was not her thing. She feared she'd be tangled in the rope in no time—and then what?

"Ready, set, jump!" called Wyatt.

Hop, hop, hippity-hop. The turning ropes became a blur, as the white rabbit jumped very fast.

Sasha had to think hard about jumping up and down. Hooves on the ground. Jump. Hooves on the ground. Jump.

"Fifty, fifty-one, fifty-two . . ." The white rabbit counted his jumps out loud. He jumped twice as fast as Sasha. Maybe even three times as fast.

Sasha wished this were a running contest. She was good at that.

"Come on, Sasha!" called Kimani.

"You can do it," cheered Wyatt.

Sasha tried to jump faster, but she couldn't. She wasn't meant to jump. She was meant to run. She was meant to fly.

That's it, thought Sasha. *I'll use my wings to help me.*

Then she remembered Wyatt said flying wasn't fair in games.

This game isn't fair, thought Sasha. *I can't win a jump rope contest against a rabbit. A galloping contest, sure. A carrot-eating contest, maybe. But not this.*

She decided to do it.

She jumped, then fluttered her wings.

She stayed in the air a second longer. But that second helped. Sasha jumped faster and faster.

Jump, flutter. Jump, flutter.

The white rabbit looked over at her. "That's not the way to jump rope."

"It's the way a flying horse jumps rope." Sasha smiled.

Jump, flutter. Jump, flutter.

"But, but . . ." The rabbit stared at her big, flapping wings. He stopped watching his rope. "Oh, no!"

His big feet got tangled in the rope. He was out.

Sasha won!

The Final Petal

"Good game." Sasha gave the white rabbit a hoof-paw bump. "So, the teal flower? You promised to show us where to find it."

"I did." He led them to a patch of seagrass. One teal flower bloomed there.

"It's blue-green," said Sasha.

"It's green-blue," said Kimani.

"It's both." Wyatt plucked a petal. They thanked the rabbit and waved goodbye. Then they flew back to the cottonwood tree in Verdant Valley.

Sasha retrieved the golden envelope and the fuchsia petal from the hidden nest. She lined up the five petals next to the envelope: fuchsia, sunburst orange, saffron yellow, lavender, and teal.

She waited.
The envelope stayed shut.
She scattered the petals on the envelope.
It still didn't open.

"I escaped from the clutches of a mountain lion, got stung by a bee, chased a speedy bird, and outjumped a rabbit to get these petals. After all that, I still don't know what this invitation says." Sasha sighed.

Then the envelope began to fade a little bit. "Quick! What should I do?" cried Sasha.

Wyatt's stomach gave a loud grumble. He blushed. "Those petals are making me hungry."

"There isn't time to feed you." Sasha pushed the disappearing envelope toward him. "Here, lick the drawing of the flower. The spicy taste will stop your hunger."

"Yuck, I don't want to—wait! I've got it!" cried Wyatt. "The petals drawn on the envelope were sticky. Remember?"

"So?" asked Kimani.

"I know what to do!" Sasha pressed the real fuchsia petal onto the drawn-on fuchsia petal. It stuck. She pressed on the sunburst orange petal, the saffron yellow petal, and the lavender petal. Then she pressed on the teal petal.

It worked! The golden envelope magically opened. A glittery invitation popped out.

Sasha read out loud:

Princess Sasha is invited to a very fancy party on the Royal Island tomorrow. Please leave now and fly there right away, so we can get you fancy for your fancy day.

At that moment, the sound of trumpets filled the air. The two silver horses streaked across the sky. Sasha felt herself being magically pulled up, up, up to them.

"We hope you and your friends enjoyed our game. You must go now," said one silver horse.

The other silver horse placed Sasha's princess crown on her head. "The King and Queen are waiting."

The first silver horse dropped wildflowers on the ground for Wyatt.

The second silver horse dropped honey-dipped carrots on the ground for Kimani.

"Thank you for helping the Lost Princess," they said. "She will be back soon."

Sasha waved her tail at her friends— then flew off to the Royal Island. It was party time!

Read on for a sneak peek
from the first book in the
Mighty Meg series!

Chapter One:
Meg's Perfectly Perfect Birthday Party

Meg's birthday was the most exciting thing to happen to her since her family went to Disneyland last summer. Turning eight was a big deal—like parades and fireworks big.

Her favorite people were there: Mom, her little brother Curtis, and her best friends Tara and Ruby. The only ones missing were Aunt Nikki and Uncle Derrick, but they would call Meg later.

Yellow balloons hung from the lights in the living room. Orange-and-red streamers looped down from the ceiling above a stack of presents on the coffee table. A three-layer cake waited in the kitchen; Meg had already peeked at the peach frosting covered in purple sprinkles. She didn't have to check the freezer to know there was a carton of rainbow sherbet inside. Her party was practically perfect.

Curtis bounced on the couch, looking more excited than Meg. But that's just how her brother acted *all* the time—like his pants were on fire.

"How much longer?" he whined.

Tara and Ruby laughed while Mom came up behind him and put her calming hands on his shoulders, settling him into the cushions. "Be patient, C. It'll just be a few more minutes."

Like Curtis, Meg couldn't understand what was taking so long. Mom kept checking her watch like they were waiting on a pizza delivery or something. But they had already eaten dinner, cleared the table, and washed the dishes.

Being eight meant that Meg was more mature than Curtis and wouldn't pester Mom over and over again about when they would open presents, no matter how much she wanted to. Still, Meg watched the clock as she pulled Tara and Ruby onto the oversized recliner with her. The girls erupted in laughter as they became a tangle of arms and legs squished together.

When the doorbell rang, Mom pretended to look shocked and said, a little too loudly, "I wonder who that is!"